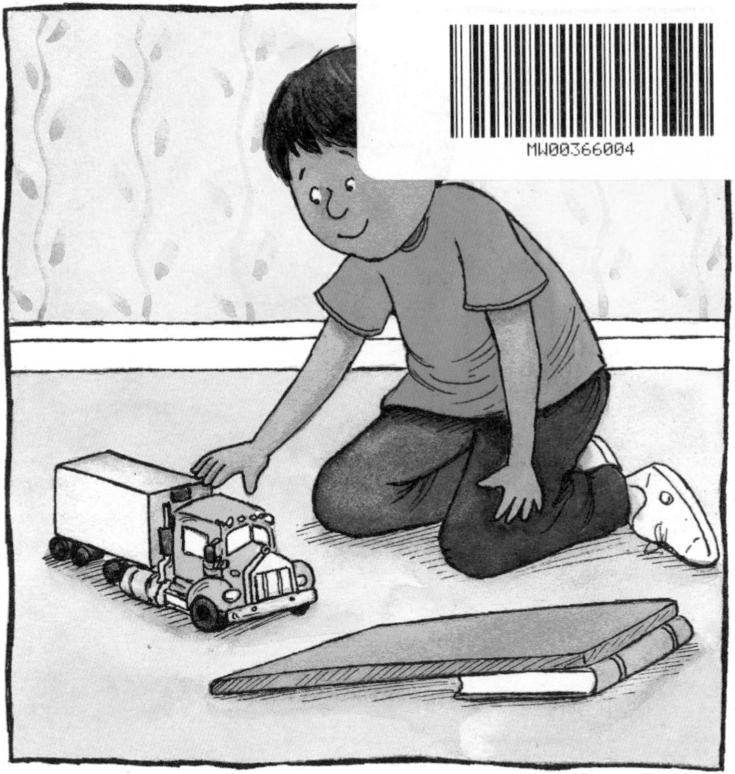

This truck is little.

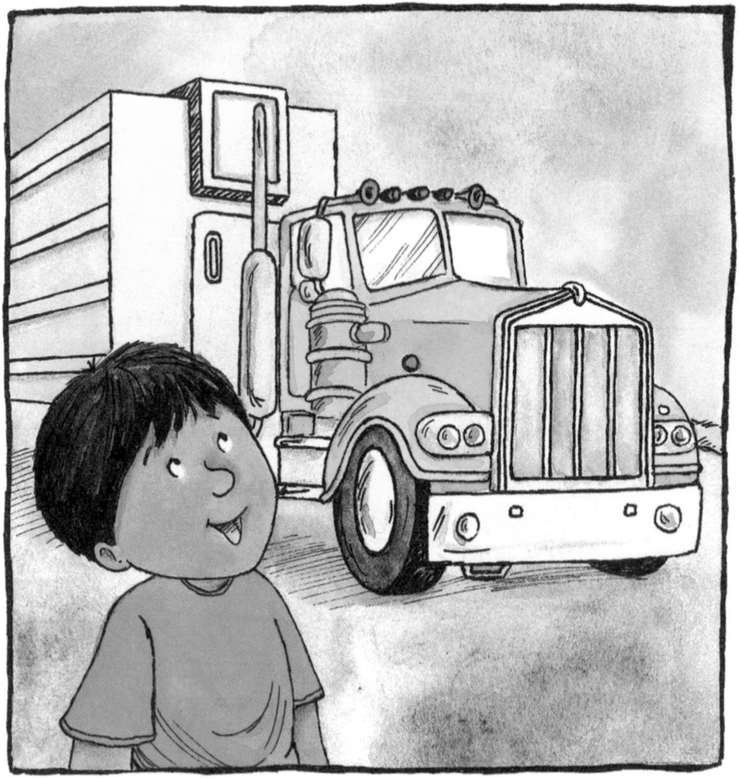

This truck is big.

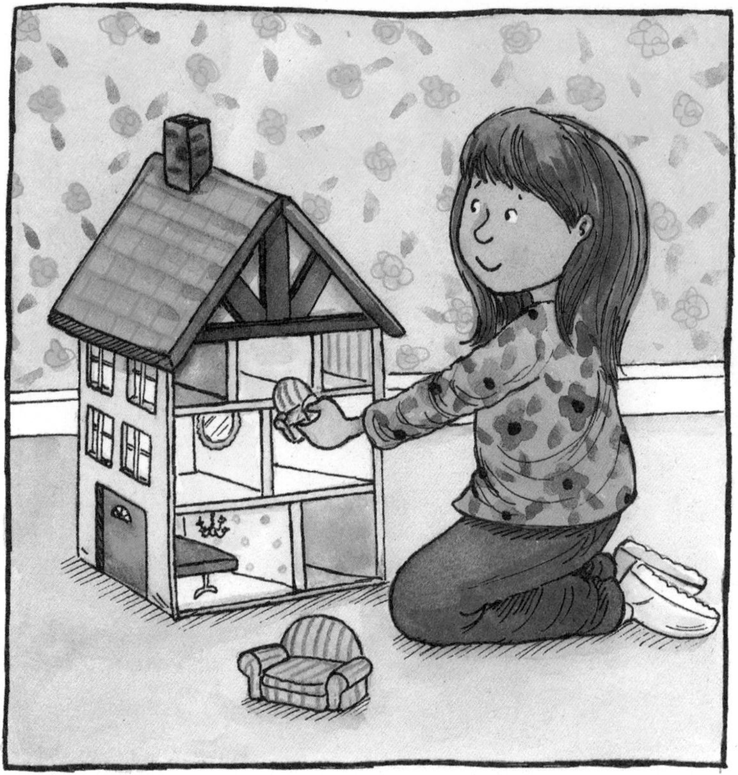

This house is little.

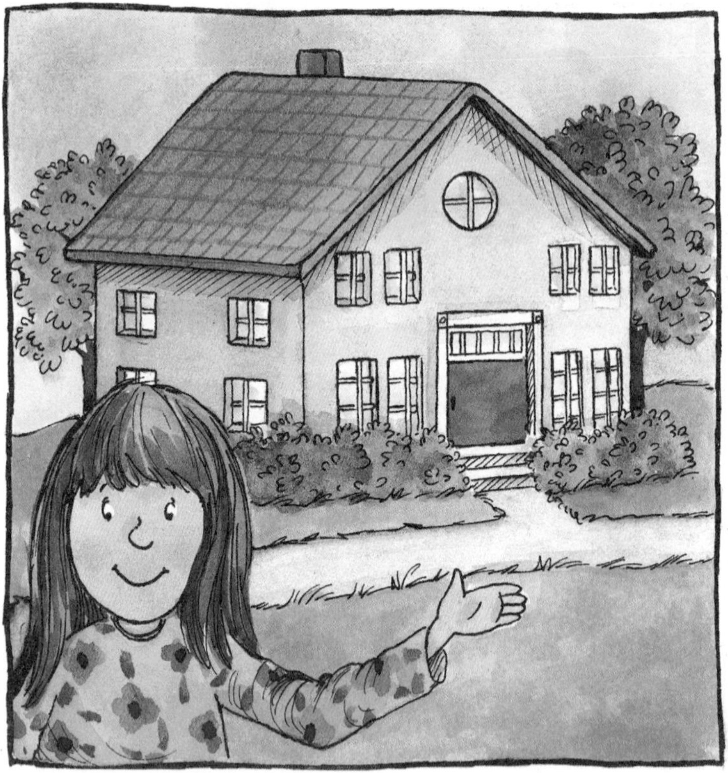

This house is big.

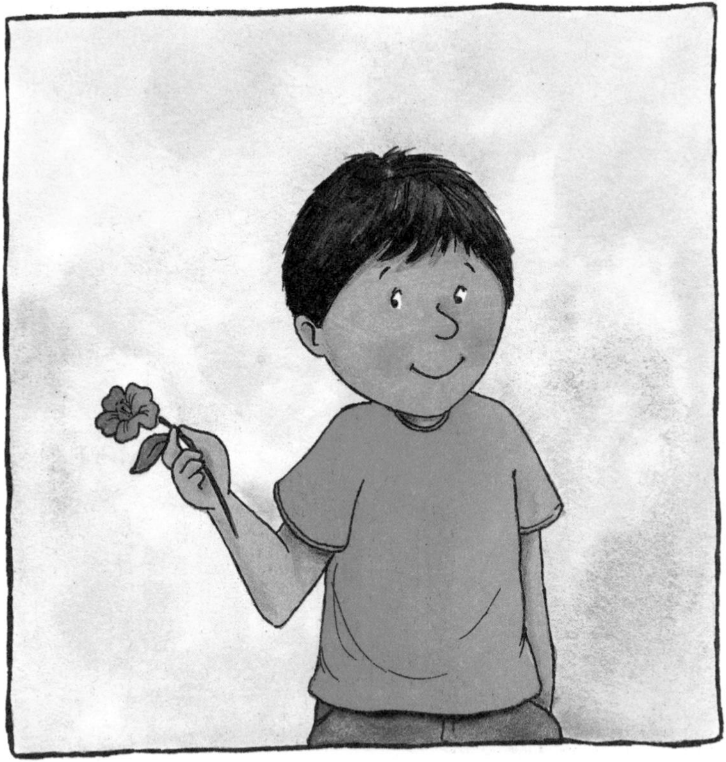

This flower is little.

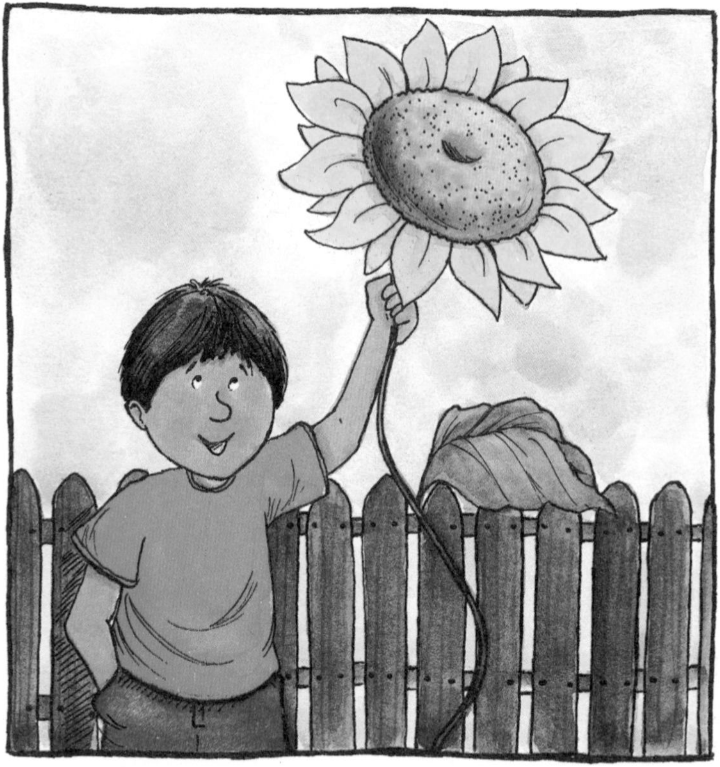

This flower is big.

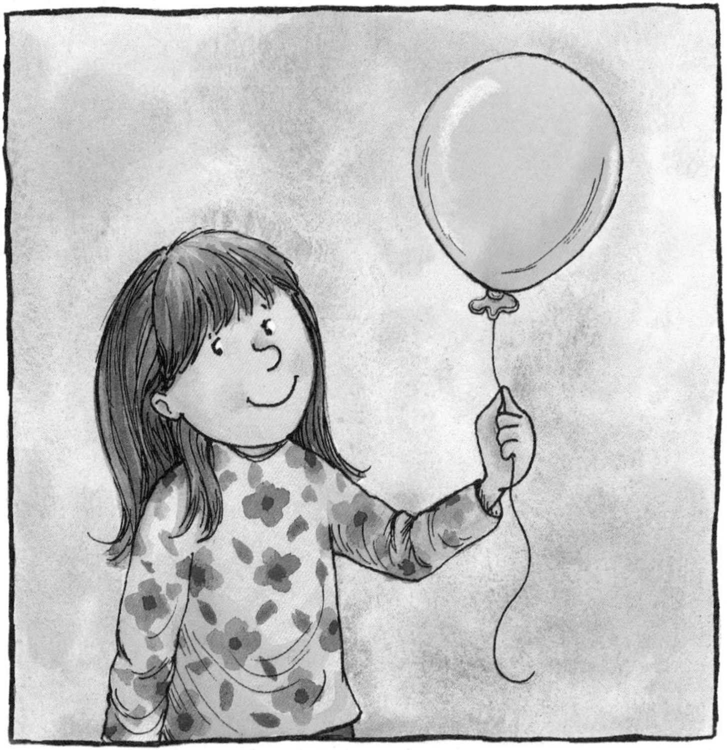

This balloon is little.

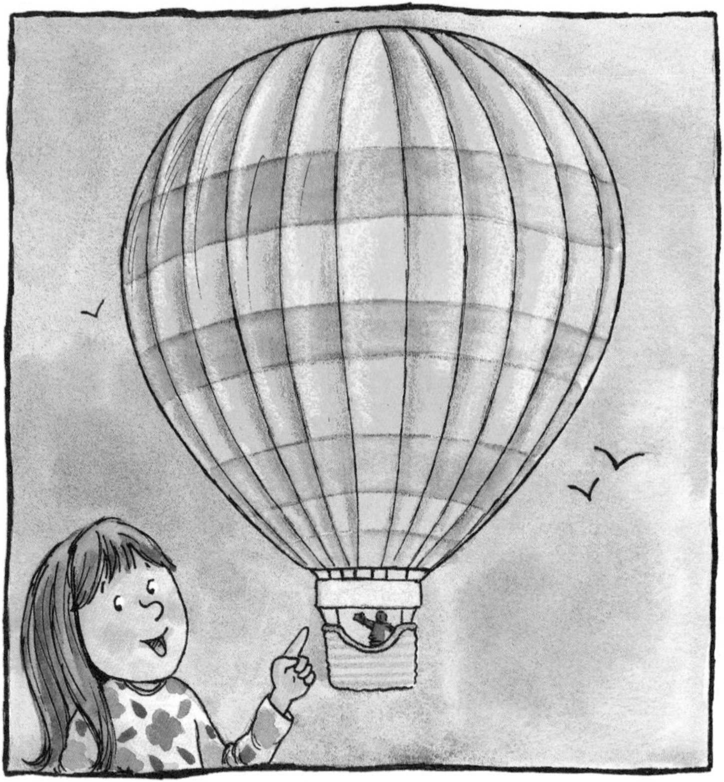

This balloon is BIG!